LOOK AND FIND

Bugs
Bunny
and Friends

Illustrated by
Jaime Diaz Studios

Illustration Script Development by
Don Dougherty

Published by Louis Weber, C.E.O.
Publications International, Ltd.
7373 North Cicero Avenue
Lincolnwood, Illinois 60646

FAMILY ENTERTAINMENT

R E A D I N G

HTS BOOKS

AN IMPRINT OF FOREST HOUSE™
School & Library Edition

It's that time of year again, and Elmer Fudd is out in the forest doing some hunting. But is it Duck Season or Rabbit Season? Could it be Elk Season or Fiddler Crab Season? Or maybe even *Baseball* Season?? With Daffy Duck outwitting Elmer, and Bugs Bunny outwitting them both, maybe nobody knows for sure. The one thing Bugs does know is that he's ready for a vacation. He's off to Pismo Beach, leaving Elmer and Daffy behind to sort things out.

Find Bugs Bunny, Elmer Fudd, and Daffy Duck, and then find the other woodland characters.

Bugs Bunny

Elmer Fudd

Daffy Duck

A great horned owl

A rainbow trout

Big Foot

A wild boar

The game warden

At first glance this looked like Pismo Beach. There's plenty of sand and plenty of sun, but not very much ocean. It looks like Bugs took a wrong turn at Albuquerque and ended up in the desert. It also looks like a certain crazed genius named Wile E. Coyote is near. He'll do anything to make Bugs the main course in a rabbit stew. Bugs shouldn't have too much trouble, though—Wile E.'s plans always backfire.

First find Bugs and Wile E. Coyote; then look for the desert characters.

Bugs Bunny

Wile E. Coyote

Captain Croissant

The Sandman

Thurston Fourwater

Oil Will

Etta Karcass

A lounge lizard

Tunneling is hard work, so Bugs popped up out West to take a carrot break. He soon found that the town he was in belonged to Yosemite Sam, and according to Sam, the town wasn't big enough for the both of them. Bugs had until sundown to get out. Now Bugs doesn't really mind being kicked out; he's on his way to Pismo Beach anyway. But you can be sure he'll teach Sam a lesson before he goes!

First find Bugs and Yosemite Sam, and then find the other Western characters.

Bugs Bunny

Yosemite Sam

General Mustard

Wyatt Twerp

Jamie Jess

Annie Oaktree

C.T. Slicker

Belle Starry

This time, Bugs thought he had arrived at Pismo Beach for sure. Just look at all the water and sunshine. But then he noticed something was missing—the beach! There was no sand anywhere. Just bridges and buildings and boats. Bugs was smack-dab in the middle of Venice, Italy, along with Tweety and Sylvester. Tweety came to enjoy a nice vacation, and Sylvester came to enjoy a nice Italian lunch . . . a pizza Tweety Pie!

See if you can find Bugs, Sylvester, and Tweety. Then find the seafaring items.

Bugs Bunny

Sylvester and Tweety

A sea serpent

A mermaid

Sinbad

The Jolly Roger

Flying fish

Octo-cop

Bugs has made wrong turns before, but this one is a doozy! If our long-eared friend is in outer space, you can be sure he'll run into Marvin the Martian. And if Marvin is around, you know he's probably trying to blow up the Earth! Don't worry though. Bugs will stop him like he always does, and then he'll be back on his way to Pismo Beach.

See if you can find Bugs and Marvin the Martian, and then look for the otherworldly characters and objects.

Bugs Bunny

Marvin the Martian

Carla Cosmonaut

Alfie Centauri

Venutian de Milo

Crash Gordon

The Rubble telescope

Bugs Bunny's spaceship

Another wrong turn and Bugs is in the jungle face-to-face with the fiercest and hungriest creature on Earth. The Tasmanian Devil loves to eat—aardvarks, beavers, rabbits, koalas, monkeys, rabbits, wildebeest, rabbits, yaks, zebras—but especially rabbits! Our carrot-eating friend had better watch his step. Bugs will enjoy Pismo Beach more if he stays in one piece.

Find Bugs Bunny and the Tasmanian Devil, and then find the jungle dwellers.

Bugs Bunny

The Tasmanian Devil

The Chief

A dandy lion

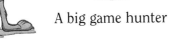

A big game hunter

Dr. Livingstone

Lady Taz

A cowala

Even after all the wild and far-out places Bugs has been to on this journey, Elmer Fudd still managed to stay on his trail. Bugs made a quick stop at this theater, figuring he could lose Elmer in the crowd. It's certainly not Pismo Beach, but Bugs can still have some fun here before he goes on his way.

Find Bugs and Elmer in the crowd, and then try to locate the theatrical characters.

Bugs Bunny

Elmer Fudd

Three Weird Sisters

Hamlet

Phantom of the Opera

Leopold

Brunhilde

Cecil B. DeMilquetoast

Bugs must be getting tired of all these wrong turns by now. But if you're gonna make a wrong turn, you might as well make one that takes you to Paris! This city is known for romance, fine foods, and sweet fragrances. One fragrance is definitely not sweet. It belongs to Pepe Le Pew, and just like always, he's chasing his true love, Penelope.

Find Bugs, Pepe Le Pew, and Penelope, and then find the French things.

Bugs Bunny

Pepe Le Pew

Penelope

Joan of Arc

A plate of escargot

A French horn

Napoleon

King Louie XIV

P ismo Beach at last!! It was quite a trip, but our globe-trotting rabbit has finally made it to his ideal vacation spot. Now Bugs can kick back and enjoy a well-earned rest! It seems an awful lot of his Looney Tunes pals have made it to the beach also.

See if you can find the other characters frolicking in the sun and sand.

Sylvester

Tasmanian Devil

Road Runner

Elmer Fudd

Yosemite Sam

Daffy Duck

Marvin the Martian

Pepe Le Pew

ACME SALT WATE

GO SHARK!

APOLLO

Daffy Duck didn't get his name by accident. This little black duck might be the wackiest waterfowl you'll ever see. See if you can find these other crazy things running loose back at the forest.

A loon
A March hare
A mad hatter
A fox
A mad scientist
Crazy Horse
Crazy eights

Wile E. Coyote has more wild gadgets than he could ever possibly use. Go back to the desert scene and find some of the things he uses to build his wacky, wiley traps.

Rocket-powered skates
"Boom"erang
A giant wooden mallet
Two-ton weight
A catapult
An anvil
A large rubber band
A giant magnet

Yosemite Sam says he's the rootinest, tootinest, goll-darn shootinest hombre north of the Rio Grande . . . and he ain't no namby-pamby either. Go to the Western town and find these other "rough and tough" guys.

Motorcycle gang
Marine drill sergeant
Tyrannosaurus rex
Sumo wrestler
Football player
Construction worker
Grizzly bear
Lumberjack

It's a sure thing Sylvester won't have Tweety for lunch, but he must have *something* to snack on. Try to find these "foods" Sylvester could enjoy for lunch along the waterways of Venice.

A submarine sandwich
A fine kettle of fish
Clam chowder
Chocolate mouse
A saucer of milk
Spaghetti
Pizza

Marvin the Martian is one guy who doesn't mess around. If he doesn't like something, he just blows it up. Go back to the outer space scene and try to find these things that blow up.

A keg of gunpowder
A stick of dynamite
A time bomb
A bazooka
A torpedo
An exploding cigar
A beach ball
Balloons

Taz is well known for the way he chomps *through* everything. Make your way back through the jungle and find these other things that can do that too.

Saber-tooth tigers
Man-eating plants
The King of the Jungle
A chain saw
A piranha
A beaver
An axe
A shark

Poor Elmer always seems to get outwitted by Bugs Bunny. He's not the only one to have a hard time with animals, though. Find these creatures that are causing trouble for someone at the theater.

Disobedient dogs
Acrobatic apes
Seals playing keep-away
A thirsty elephant
A chicken hawk with a net
Fruit-snatching monkeys
A pirating parrot
A love-struck cow

Pepe Le Pew is one love-struck skunk! He's always got romance on his mind, and he never gives up the chase. See if you can find these romantic things in Paris.

Bouquet of red flowers
Cupid
Heart-shaped box of candy
Bride
A couple kissing
Love letters
A couple sharing a soda
A marriage proposal

What's up, Doc? After all that traveling, Bugs is ready for a tasty little snack. See if you can find these treats that our wascally wabbit might enjoy at the beach.

Carrot cake
Carrot juice
Chocolate-covered carrots
Carrot-on-a-stick
Barbecued carrots
Carrot sandwich
Carrot-kabobs
Toasted carrots